Look Out, Fox!

Written by Jill Eggleton
Illustrated by Bregje van Pallandt

"This is my hole,"
said Mole.

Mole's hole

“This is my hole,”
said Rat.

Mole's hole
Rat's hole

"This is my hole,"
said Rabbit.

Mole's hole
Rat's hole
Rabbit's hole

“This is my hole,”
said Fox.

Fox's hole
Rat's hole
Mole's hole
Rabbit's

Fox's hole
Rat's hole

“Yuck!
This is not my hole,”
said Fox.

Signs
Mole's hole
Rat's hole
Rabbit's hole

Fox's
hole

Guide Notes

Title: Look Out, Fox!
Stage: Emergent – Magenta

Genre: Fiction
Approach: Guided Reading
Processes: Thinking Critically, Exploring Language, Processing Information
Written and Visual Focus: Signs
Word Count: 32

Reading the Text

Tell the children that the story is about a mole, a rat, a rabbit, and a fox. The mole, rat, and rabbit find a good hole to live in, but the fox wants to live there, too.
Talk to them about what is on the front cover. Read the title and the author / illustrator.
"Walk" through the book, focusing on the illustrations and talking to the children about what is happening on each page.
Before looking at pages 12 - 13, ask the children to make a prediction.
Read the text together.

Thinking Critically
(sample questions)

- Why do you think the animals liked the hole?
- What do you think will happen to the hole after the fox leaves?

Exploring Language
(ideas for selection)

Terminology
Title, cover, author, illustrator, illustrations

Vocabulary
Interest words: hole, mole, rat, rabbit, fox
High-frequency words: is, my, said

Print Conventions
Capital letter for sentence beginnings and names (**M**ole, **R**at, **R**abbit, **F**ox), periods